The Pirate Code

First published in 2011
by Wayland

Wayland
338 Euston Road
London NW1 3BH

Wayland Australia
Level 17/207 Kent Street
Sydney, NSW 2000

Series Editor: Louise John
Editor: Katie Woolley
Cover design: Paul Cherrill
Design: D.R.ink
Consultant: Shirley Bickler

A CIP catalogue record for this book is available from the British Library.

ISBN 9780750264945

Printed in China

Wayland is a division of Hachette Children's Books,
an Hachette UK Company

www.hachette.co.uk

The Pirate Code

Written by Tom Easton
Illustrated by Matt Buckingham

WAYLAND

It was a hot, quiet day. The Stuck Pig bobbed gently on the calm sea. On board, the Poor Pirates and Long John's parrot were fast asleep, snoring.

Big Ben, the lookout, was having such a nice dream about blueberries and cream that he didn't notice another ship sailing towards the Stuck Pig.

It was Captain Greenbeard and his ship, the Hard Cheese, sailed by five of the meanest pirates on the Seven Seas.

Long John's parrot woke up and gave a loud squawk, just as the Hard Cheese pulled alongside. But it was too late!

The Mean Pirates swung aboard and, as quick as a flash, Captain Flint's sleepy crew were tied up like shoelaces.

“What’s all this?” the Captain roared. “Cut us loose, Greenbeard.”

Greenbeard laughed. “Sorry, Flint,” he replied. “I have other plans!”

The Mean Pirates launched a jolly boat and, one by one, lowered the Poor Pirates into it.

"The Stuck Pig is a bit old and leaky," Greenbeard called down. "But once it's back at port, I'm sure someone will buy it for a good price."

"You can't do that!" Selma shouted back. "What about the Pirate Code? You're not supposed to steal from other pirates."

"You're the worst pirates ever to sail the seas," Greenbeard cried. "The other pirates will thank us for taking your ship away."

And, with that, Greenbeard and his crew sailed off, towing the Stuck Pig behind them.

Selma began to pull at her ropes with her teeth. Eventually she managed to wriggle free and untie the other pirates.

“Squawk, well done, Selma,” Long John’s parrot said.

“But what good does it do us?” Pegleg Pete cried. “We’re still stuck in this jolly boat.”

“And it’s getting cold and dark,” Big Ben pointed out. “I’m scared.”

“Don’t worry everyone,” the Captain said. “I’ve had a **brilliant** idea.”

The Captain set about lighting a fire to keep everyone warm. It crackled merrily as Pegleg Pete dropped another bit of broken oar onto it.

"Captain?" Selma said.

"What is it, Selma?" the Captain replied cheerfully, as he warmed his hands.

"What's going to stop the fire from burning a hole in the bottom of the boat?" she asked.

"It's already happening!" squealed Long John's Parrot.

"Quick, put some water onto the fire, now!" cried the Captain.

But it was too late. The fire had burnt a hole in the bottom of the boat and the crew were sinking... fast!

The pirates were very cross with the Captain.

“Don’t blame me, it’s Big Ben’s fault we’re in this mess,” the Captain said. “He should have spotted the Mean Pirates coming.”

“Actually, Captain,” Selma said, glaring at Pegleg Pete. “It was Pete’s turn to be on lookout but he didn’t wake Ben because he was asleep, too.”

"It wasn't my turn!" Pete cried. "It was Long John's turn. We swapped last week, remember?"

Long John shrugged, but his parrot spoke up. “Squawk! The Captain said swapping wasn’t allowed and that it was still your turn.”

"Well he didn't tell me!" Pegleg Pete shouted.

By now, the pirates were knee-deep in the ocean. Everyone turned to look at the Captain who glared back angrily.

"I told Arthur to tell you," the Captain spluttered. "It's all Arthur's fault!"

"Come to think of it. Where is Arthur?" asked Selma, peering under an oar.

The pirates looked everywhere, but Arthur was nowhere to be seen.

"Arthur!" the Captain roared. "Where are you?"

"Here I am, Captain!" cried Arthur from somewhere behind them.

And there, in the light of the moon, was Arthur Sandwich, standing alone on the deck of the Stuck Pig.

"Hurrah!" the Poor Pirates all cried.

"But how did you get back onto the Stuck Pig?" asked the Captain, when they'd climbed back on board their ship.

"Simple," Arthur replied, "I never left. I was asleep in the hold when the Mean Pirates sailed off. I came up on deck and cut the tow rope.

"But how ever did you find us in this great ocean?" Selma asked.

"I followed the Captain's signal,"
Arthur replied.

They all turned to look at the Captain, who blushed with embarrassment.

"Setting fire to the jolly boat," Arthur said, winking. "Now that really was a **brilliant** idea, Captain!"

START READING is a series of highly enjoyable books for beginner readers. **The books have been carefully graded to match the Book Bands widely used in schools.** This enables readers to be sure they choose books that match their own reading ability.

Look out for the Band colour on the book in our Start Reading logo.

The Bands are:

START READING books can be read independently or shared with an adult. They promote the enjoyment of reading through satisfying stories, plays and non-fiction narratives, which are supported by fun illustrations and photographs.

Tom Easton lives in Surrey, works in London and spends a lot of time travelling between the two, which is when he does his writing. Tom has written books for children, teenagers and adults, under a variety of pseudonyms. He has three children and is looking forward to having macaroni cheese tonight.

Matt Buckingham would have rather liked a job as a pirate if he hadn't become an illustrator. The only problem is Matt gets seasick, so it's probably best if he sticks to drawing pirates instead.